Famous!

DAVID MORTIMORE BAXTER

by Karen Tayleur

illustrated by Brann Garvey

STONE ARCH BOOKS
www.stonearchbooks.com

David Mortimore Baxter is published by Stone Arch Books
151 Good Counsel Drive, P.O. Box 669
Mankato, Minnesota 56002
www.stonearchbooks.com

Library of Congress Cataloging-in-Publication Data
Tayleur, Karen.
    Famous: The Awesome Life of David Mortimore Baxter / by Karen Tayleur;
illustrated by Brann Garvey.
      p. cm. — (David Mortimore Baxter)
      ISBN 978-1-4342-1196-5 (library binding)
      [1. Reality television programs—Fiction. 2. Mothers—Fiction. 3. Family
life—Fiction.] I. Garvey, Brann, ill. II. Title.
PZ7.T21149Fam 2009
[Fic]—dc22   2008031573

Summary:
David thinks the coolest thing in the world would be to be on TV. So why isn't he
more excited when his family is chosen to be filmed for the hit reality show Trading
Moms? When he finds out whose family the Baxters will be trading moms with, it's
even worse...the other mom is the mother of his biggest enemy, Rose Thornton!
Being on TV might be cool, but this isn't fun at all.

Creative Director: Heather Kindseth
Graphic Designer: Carla Zetina-Yglesias

Photo Credits
Delaney Photography, cover

1 2 3 4 5 6 14 13 12 11 10 09

Table of Contents

chapter 1
The Coolest Thing 5

chapter 2
Experiment 12

chapter 3
Rose Thornton's Mother? 20

chapter 4
Rose's Plan 27

chapter 5
Day One 33

chapter 6
Just Wait 41

chapter 7
The Worst Day 48

chapter 8
Thornton's Rules 55

chapter 9
Disaster! 62

chapter 10
Sick Of It 70

chapter 11
The Prize 78

THE COOLEST THING

Joe and I were stuck at my house because I was grounded.

It wasn't even my fault. I mean, I know I was supposed to be collecting money for the Bays Park Historical Society. **Gran** had come over during the weekend. She shoved a collection can into my hand and asked me to collect money in my neighborhood. **It was for a good cause.**

I meant to help. I went outside, planning to go ask my neighbors for money for the Historical Society. But when I went outside, **Joe** and **Bec** were there. I thought I'd hang out with them for a little while. So I put the collection can down, and then I sort of FORGOT about it.

Anyway, I'm not sure that **Joe** should have been at our house since I was grounded. But Mom never said I couldn't have friends over, so **I figured it was okay.**

But I couldn't leave my house, so Joe and I were ⓑⓞⓡⓔⓓ. We were just sitting around.

"What do you think **the coolest thing in the world** is?" Joe asked me.

I had to think hard about that. I mean, it would be cool to have a **million dollars**. But that's probably not the coolest thing in the world. And it would be cool to own a chocolate store, but you might end up getting sick of eating chocolate, which would not be so cool.

I've always thought it would be cool to **be on TV**. I like the idea of strangers coming up to me on the street and asking, "Didn't I see you on TV?"

If they wanted an ⒶⓊⓉⓄⒼⓇⒶⓅⒽ, I would probably give them one. I've even been practicing my signature, just in case I might need to autograph something some day.

David Mortimore Baxter

There are lots of shows on TV that I could be on. There's a show on after school called *Skool Quiz*, which is only for kids, but I don't think I would like to go on that. You have to answer questions like you're at school or something. **That would be boring.**

Then there's *Name That Song*. My sister, Zoe, would be **really good** at that show, because she's always listening to music. I can never remember the words of songs so I probably wouldn't go on that show.

Then there's *Stayin' Alive*. On that show, contestants have to go on an island and SURVIVE using whatever they can find, without supplies or tents or anything.

I told Joe we should try out for that show. Joe said I wouldn't last two days without my comfy bed. Then I said that he wouldn't last an hour without his DVD player. Then he said I wouldn't last a minute without a television and after that **things got really ugly**.

We were still trading INSULTS when Dad asked us to be quiet because he was on the phone. I could have reminded him that it was a cordless phone and he could move to another room, but **I'm not that stupid**.

Dad was doing that thing he does when something is **really serious**. He had a little frown on his face and he kept nodding, even though the person on the other end of the phone couldn't see him.

"Uh huh, uh huh," he said about ten times.

Something SERIOUS was going on. I was sure of it, because when Dad got off the phone I asked him what was going on and he just said he needed to talk to Mom. She was out shopping, so Dad went into the computer room and shut the door.

Then Joe and I started thinking about all the things that it could be.

"Maybe the people at NASA want your dad to go up in the next **space shuttle**," said Joe.

I shook my head. Dad was some kind of scientist, not an astronaut.

"Maybe the CIA wants him to be a SPY," said Joe.

"Maybe," I said. But that sounded like something that might happen in a **movie**, not in **real life**.

"Maybe it was Ms. Stacey," Joe said.

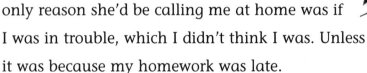

Ms. Stacey was my teacher at school. The only reason she'd be calling me at home was if I was in trouble, which I didn't think I was. Unless it was because my homework was late.

But **my homework was always late**. I didn't think she'd be calling about that.

I was still busy **worrying** about the whole Ms. Stacey late homework thing when **Mom** finally got home.

"Can we help bring in the groceries, Mom?" I said. She looked a little 𝕄𝔸𝔻 because Joe was there. "Oh, by the way, Dad was looking for you," I added.

"Okay," Mom said, looking around.

"He's in the computer room," I said. Then Joe and I headed outside.

We were lifting bags of groceries out of Mom's car when **I suddenly heard her yell**.

"What?" Mom screamed.

Joe looked at me. "Did you hear that?" he asked.

I nodded. "I think the **whole neighborhood** heard that," I said.

"I think I might go home," said **Joe**. He shoved his bag of groceries on top of the one I was already holding. Then he **scooted** down the street.

When I was done with the groceries, I found **Zoe**, standing in front of the computer room door.

"What's going on?" I whispered.

"Ssshhh," she said.

Then my brother, Harry, came out of his room. He asked us what was going on.

"**We don't know,**" I said.

"Ssshhh," said Zoe.

"Well, why don't you *ask*?" asked **Harry**.

Then Boris, my dog, **waddled** up the hallway. He licked me on the hand.

"Cut that out," I whispered.

Boris barked.

"Ssshhh," said Zoe.

Boris barked again. That was his way of saying, "I don't have to be *quiet* if I don't want to."

Then Zoe got mad and said, "Sssshhhh" again. Boris just barked back and Harry started **whining** about being hungry. Finally, the door opened. Dad stood in the doorway and we all got quiet.

"What's going on?" **Dad** asked.

"That's what we want to know," said Harry.

"Let's all go into the living room," said Dad.

So we all went into the living room. Zoe, Harry, and I sat on the couch. Boris sat on my feet. Then Dad and Mom came into the room. Usually **Mom** does all the talking, but she just stood there looking ANGRY.

Dad looked at all of us. Then he said, **"How would you feel about the Baxter family being on TV?"**

CHAPTER 2

EXPERIMENT

Everyone started talking at the same time. Well, **everyone except Mom,** that is.

Harry was shouting out how **cool** it would be and Zoe was saying that she didn't have anything to wear. I was trying to find out when it was going to happen and Boris was barking because that's what Boris does.

Finally, Mom clapped her hands and we got $QUIET$ again.

"Okay," Mom said. "One at a time."

"All right," said **Dad**.

He pointed to me. "To answer you first, David, this could happen in the next couple of weeks. If everything goes as planned," Dad said.

Then he pointed to Zoe. "Zoe, as far as I'm aware, you would just be wearing your **regular** clothes. Whatever is in your closet, or on your floor," he added with a smile.

Zoe scowled and muttered something about needing at least **ten new outfits** if she was going to be on TV.

Then Dad pointed to Harry. "Yes, I think it will be **cool**, Harry," Dad said. He looked at Mom and added, "Your mom doesn't seem to think it's a good idea, though."

"You 𝓗𝓐𝓣𝓔 TV, Thomas," said Mom. "And if you do watch it, you only watch documentaries."

"That's not true, Cordelia," said Dad. "I watch other shows too."

"Really?" said Mom. "What shows? Name one."

"There's that show about detectives," said Dad. "You know, the one with **that smart guy**."

"Yes?" prompted Mom.

"Well, I don't know what it's called," said Dad.

"What's the show about, Dad?" I asked. "The one we're going to be on."

"It's a social conditioning 𝑬𝑿𝑷𝑬𝑹𝑰𝑴𝑬𝑵𝑻, conducted under strict guidelines," said Dad.

Experiment? I imagined myself being stuck to a slide and put under a *microscope*. Or lying on a table and being operated on by a **mad scientist**. Or stuck in a test tube and SHAKEN around.

No wonder Dad wanted to be on the TV show. He was a scientist. He'd love it.

Mom snorted again. "It's a reality show," she said.

"Reality show?" said Zoe.

"It sounds bad when you put it like that, Cordelia," said Dad.

"I'm **sorry**, but that's what it is," Mom said.

"Reality show?" said Harry. "Like *Search for a Star* or something?"

"That's a talent show," I said. "A reality show is more like *Stayin' Alive.*"

"Whoa. I am not going to live on an island with a whole bunch of people I don't know. I'm not eating **disgusting** things that should never crawl out from under the rocks they live under," said Zoe. "I hate camping. HATE. You know that, Dad. How could you think I would want to do this?"

"It's not a survival reality show," said Dad.

"Is it one of those cooking reality shows?" I asked. "You know, one of the shows where the chef in charge is **really rude** and tells everyone how awful they are at their job and then the winner ends up with a restaurant?"

I was never allowed to watch that show.

"No," said Mom.

"It's nothing that RIDICULOUS," said Dad. "You will hardly even know the cameras are here."

"Here?" said Zoe.

"It's Trading Moms," said Mom firmly.

Trading Moms? The name sounded familiar.

"Isn't that the show where the mom goes to a **different** family?" asked Harry.

"Yes," said Mom.

"So you would have to move to another house and we would have **another mother**?" I asked.

"Cameras in my room?" said Zoe. "No way."

"But I don't want to **trade moms**," yelled **Harry**. "No way."

"It's only for two weeks," said Dad.

"No way," I said. I didn't want some stranger coming into my home and telling me what I could and couldn't do. It was **bad enough** when my own parents did that.

"I think it could be fun," said Dad.

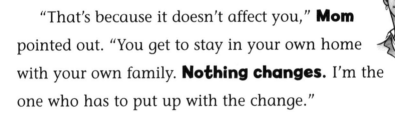

"That's because it doesn't affect you," **Mom** pointed out. "You get to stay in your own home with your own family. **Nothing changes.** I'm the one who has to put up with the change."

"We will **ALL** be affected," said Dad. "We will have to live under the rules of the other mother in the second week of the show. We will have to go along with **whatever she decides to do**."

"So why bother doing it?" asked Zoe. "Being on TV is going to turn me into the school freak."

"Yeah, it's not like they're giving us **a million dollars** or anything," said Harry.

Dad scratched his head. "Oh, didn't I mention the **money**?" he asked. "There's money involved. As long as each family lasts for two weeks, there's a **prize**."

All of a sudden it didn't seem like such a bad idea. I could last two weeks with a new mom. **How hard could it be?**

"How much of a prize, Dad?" I asked.

"Fifty thousand dollars," he said.

"Fifty thousand?" repeated Mom.

Dad nodded.

Suddenly we were all talking again. Zoe thought that maybe it wouldn't be too hard to put up with. Harry wanted to call his best friend, Sammy, to let him know **we were going to be on TV.**

"Can Boris stay?" I asked.

"Everything stays the same," said Dad. "Except that we trade your mother for someone else. What do you say, Cordelia? It will be an 𝔸𝔻𝕍𝔼ℕ𝕋𝕌ℝ𝔼."

"An adventure," repeated Mom. "Fifty thousand dollars?"

Dad nodded.

"It seems to me that I am the one with the most to lose from this show," said Mom. "So I should get to say what we spend the money on. **Is that a deal?**"

"It's a deal," said Dad, before anyone else could say anything.

"Okay," she said. "I'm in."

It wasn't until much later, after Dad called the TV producers to tell them we were in, that we bothered to ask about the *other family*.

"I hope we get a young mother," said Zoe. "Not that you're not 𝕐𝕆𝕌ℕ𝔾, Mom," she added quickly.

"I hope she can **cook**," said Harry. "And make my school lunches the right way, like you do."

"Do you know who the other family is, Dad?" I asked.

I figured we wouldn't know them, so I was a little 𝕊𝕌ℝℙℝ𝕀𝕊𝔼𝔻 when Dad nodded.

"Sure do," he said. "So **it shouldn't be too hard.**"

"So who is the other family?" I asked.

"We're trading with some **very dear friends** of ours," said Dad.

"Who?" I asked.

Dad smiled and said, "We're trading with the Thornton family. You know, **Rose Thornton's mother.**"

CHAPTER 3

ROSE THORNTON'S MOTHER?

For those of you who don't know me, let's just say that **Rose Thornton** is the one person in my life who I really, really don't like. I am not allowed to hate her, because Mom says I shouldn't hate anyone.

"We can't do it," I said. "Anyone but Rose Thornton's mom."

"Rose's mom is pretty cool," said Zoe.

"But she's Rose Thornton's mom," I said. "No way, we can't. We just can't."

Dad shook his head. He said it was *too late*. He'd already signed a form and sent it to the producers, because they'd wanted an answer that night. He said it was COMPLICATED.

I didn't see what was so complicated. If we didn't want to do it we shouldn't have to. I mean, that's what living in a **free country** is all about.

I tried to talk to Harry about it, but he was too busy talking on the phone to his friend Sammy.

Zoe had her door shut. She didn't answer when **I knocked about a gazillion times.** She was probably on her computer telling all her friends about the new outfits she was going to buy.

I found Mom in the kitchen making dinner. I was expecting her to be grumpy or a little sad at least, but she was humming. She even had a little SMILE on her face.

"So, you're okay with this, Mom?" I asked.

She nodded.

"We can't back out of it now?" I asked.

She shook her head. "I think it will be interesting," she said. "What was Joe doing here this afternoon? You were grounded."

I'd forgotten all about that.

"Um, we were just doing some homework," I said.

Mom said, "Being grounded means no friends over. **Is that clear, David?**"

"Yes, Mom," I mumbled.

"Good," she said. "Because if that happens again, **you will be grounded for a week!**"

I was starting to think that having a new mother for two weeks might not be such a BAD thing. I went to my room and shut the door. Then I had to open it again when **Boris** scratched at it.

"Come in, boy," I said.

We stayed there until dinner.

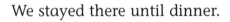

Over the next couple of days, it felt like there was a lot going on at home that I didn't know about. When Dad was home he was always in the computer room with the door shut. Mom kept having meetings with strangers in the dining room and making me use my MANNERS whenever they spoke to me.

I just tried to stay **out of the way** and hung out with **Joe** and **Bec** after school. I wanted to stay away from home.

Even school wasn't normal.

Rose Thornton usually doesn't talk to me, which is **fine with me.** But now she kept looking at me in class and whispering to her friends. Or walking slowly past my desk like she was listening in to my conversations. It was obvious that **Rose was not happy.** She wasn't happy with the thought of having my mother living at her house. And she wasn't happy that it was going to be broadcast all over the world.

Bec said that Rose was probably just as unhappy as I was about the whole thing. But Joe and I doubted it. Rose loved attention. How much more attention could you get than being on TV? **I was just surprised Rose hadn't told the entire school.**

On the fourth day of the whispering and walking past, Rose dropped a note on my desk. I thought she was dropping *garbage*.

"Hey, Rose, you dropped something," I said loudly.

Rose had already sat down at her desk. She was staring hard at me, and her eyebrows were going up and down **like a caterpillar doing push-ups.**

I waved the paper in the air. "Here," I said. "You dropped this."

Rose continued the eyebrow movement while her face turned DEEP RED.

"What is wrong with her?" I asked Joe.

"It's that paper," said Joe. "I think it might be a **note**."

A note? From Rose Thornton? I unfolded the paper and saw Rose's handwriting in purple pen.

It said, **"Meet me at the library. Biography section. Lunchtime. Come alone."**

Lunch is my favorite time of the school day. I didn't want to spend it hanging around the library with Rose Thornton. What if someone saw me? **What if someone thought Rose liked me?** I mentioned that to Joe, but he shrugged.

"No one would ever think that," he said. "As if Rose Thornton would go out with you."

If anyone else had said that, I might just be ANNOYED. But **Joe Pagnopolous** is my best friend in the world. I knew what he meant.

I think.

* * *

At lunchtime, Joe and Bec went to hang out at our **favorite spot** under the oak tree. I told them I'd meet up with them after I talked to Rose. Then I went to the library.

I looked around for Rose Thornton but couldn't see her anywhere. Maybe it was all a J☉KE. Maybe she was just setting me up.

I finally asked someone where the biography section was. They pointed out an aisle not too far away. I walked down the aisle, but **I didn't see Rose anywhere.** I picked out a book and started looking at the pictures.

"Psssst," I heard.

I looked around, but I couldn't see anyone.

"Pssst."

I went to put the book back on the shelf and noticed **an eye** looking at me from the other side of the shelf.

It was Rose Thornton.

I was going to ask her what was going on. Then she said **the only thing in her life** that I have ever agreed with.

"This *Trading Moms* show has to stop," she growled. "Right ."

CHAPTER 4

Rose and I talked through the library shelf about what we could do.

Rose's mother worked in PR. That meant she did something with 𝕋𝕍 and 𝕊𝕋𝔸ℝ𝕊.  So Rose knew a lot about what went on behind the scenes on reality shows.

"It's all in the **editing**," said Rose. "It doesn't matter what really happens. They can chop up the truth and make you look **really bad**."

"Who can?" I asked.

"The editors," said Rose. "It's all about ratings and advertising. I'll end up **the biggest joke** of Bays Park." She sighed. "I wish my mom had never signed us up," she added.

Rose explained that her mom was friends with one of the show's producers.

"What does a **producer** do, anyway?" I asked.

I saw Rose's eye blink through the gap. "A producer is the one with the **idea** and the **money**," she said. "**Everyone knows that.** Anyway, that's how we got involved."

"Well, I don't want to be involved," I said.

I didn't mind the idea of being on TV. What I minded was having a different mother for two weeks. Mrs. Thornton was **okay**, but she wasn't my mom.

What if Mom liked it better at the Thornton house? Maybe she wouldn't want to come home.

"So what are you going to do?" said Rose.

"Me?" I yelled. "*It's your mom's fault.* You're the one who should do something about it," I added more quietly.

"We should both think of a plan," said Rose.

We agreed to meet the next day, same place, same time. I shoved the book back into the gap on the shelf and waited for Rose to leave the library.

Finally, I understood why Rose was keeping *Trading Moms* a secret.

* * *

No one knew about *Trading Moms* at lunchtime, but everyone knew by the end of the day. Someone had hung up signs all over school.

I found out when **Jordan Farmer** waved one of the signs in front of my nose. "Hey, David, you didn't tell me you were going to be on TV," he said.

I grabbed the sign away from him. "It's a mistake," I mumbled.

I found out later that Rose Thornton had told her friends about the show but she'd sworn them to secrecy. Then she'd had a fight with Alysha Devine, who decided to spill the beans and put up the signs as revenge.

A bunch of kids called me that night. I had to take the phone off the hook and hope that Mom didn't notice.

We were eating dinner when there was a knock at the front door.

"I'll get it," I said, pushing my plate aside
and running to the door.

When I opened the door I found a very
angry Rose Thornton standing there, tapping
her feet.

"What are you doing here?" I asked. "It isn't
Trading Kids." I laughed because I thought it
was a good joke, but Rose just **frowned**.

"There is something wrong with your phone," she
said. "I have been trying to call you for an hour."

I didn't bother telling her about the phone off the
hook, because I was pretty sure that would only make
her *madder*. "How did you get here?" I asked.

"Dad's waiting in the car," Rose said. "I said I had
to talk to you about some homework."

"What homework?" I asked.

"I just **made it up**," said Rose. "Listen, I think I
know how to get out of this show. I think we should
just be as horrible as we can be. I mean, really be
awful. I think we should be so **AWFUL** that they
can't possibly put us on TV."

I wanted to say that **Rose didn't need to act awful because she already was**, but I kept that joke to myself.

"Well, do you have any **better** ideas?" Rose demanded.

I shook my head.

"Didn't think so," she said.

Then she told me something terrible. It was something that made my stomach bounce down to my toes and back again.

A car horn honked from the driveway.

"I better go," Rose said.

I went back to the dining room.

"Who was at the door, David?" asked **Dad**.

I explained that Rose had needed help with some homework. Zoe made a face at me like she didn't believe me. Then Mom brought in a special dessert. **Chocolate cake.**

"Cordelia, that looks **delicious**," said Dad.

"Well, I wanted tonight's meal to be SPECIAL," said Mom, placing the large plate in the middle of the table.

"Is it your *anniversary* or something?" **Harry** asked.

"That's in September," said Zoe. "What's up, Mom?"

"I know," I said. I hadn't bothered to sit back down in my seat. "Rose told me. ***Trading Moms starts tomorrow.***"

CHAPTER 5

The next morning we had to get up **really early** because the production people were coming. The production people were the cameramen and sound people and a **bunch** of other people.

"Just pretend we're not here," one lady named **Irini** kept saying.

She seemed to be the one in charge, because when she talked, everyone paid attention. Except me, of course.

When Irini asked everyone to stay out of the living room, I walked through **brushing my teeth.** When she asked everyone to line up on the front doorstep, I DISAPPEARED to the garage. It took them forever to find me.

Finally, **Dad** pulled me aside and asked me what the **problem** was.

"I don't want to do this," I said.

"Well, that's **too bad**," he said. Then he marched me out to the doorstep where I had to smile and pretend I was happy.

Then we had to wave GOODBYE to Mom as she drove out the driveway and **left us.** She actually had to do this a couple of times.

The first time, Mr. McCafferty, our neighbor, just happened to be walking by. Irini said he walked in front of the camera. The second time, **Boris** decided to lie down right by the car and it took at least **five people** to pick him up and move him.

Finally, Mom drove out of the driveway. Then she stopped down the street, because she wasn't *really* *leaving* yet.

Then things happened really quickly. We helped Mom carry her suitcases and Dad loaded up the car and suddenly **she was really gone.**

She was only moving across town, but it felt like she was going for good.

I waved goodbye from the driveway. "Bye, Mom," I yelled.

"Get a close-up on that, Camera One," I heard Irini say.

I looked up to see a camera pointing my way. **I stuck my tongue out.**

"Cut," said Irini. **"Nice work, David,"** she said ruffling my hair.

I **HATE** it when people do that.

* * *

I found out that Mrs. Thornton was supposed to be at our house when I got home from school.

At school, Rose dropped another note on my desk and we met at the library at lunchtime.

To:
DAVID

"How did this morning go?" she asked.

I shrugged.

"It wasn't as bad as I thought," Rose said. "One of the camera guys is this guy named Roger. He said I have **really nice teeth.** And my mother got me a new TV for my room, so I wouldn't miss her too much."

I didn't even have an **OLD** TV in my room.

"Anyway, it's only for two weeks," Rose said. "I mean, today is practically over. So that's only thirteen days left. So I just wanted to let you know that I'm okay with it. The whole *Trading Moms* thing."

"Oh, well. As long as you're **okay**, I guess," I said, using my most **sarcastic** voice.

"Exactly," said Rose.

* * *

For once, I wasn't really looking forward to going **home** from school. I slipped in through the back door, but I ran right into Zoe, who was carrying a basket into the laundry room.

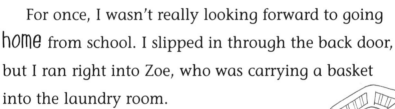

"Is she here?" I asked.

"If you mean **Mrs. Thornton**, no," said Zoe. "The cameras won't be back until tonight."

"What's for dinner?" I asked.

"I don't know," **Zoe** said. "Mrs. Thornton is cooking dinner. She's supposed to do things **our way** this week and **her way** next week. Someone dropped off her stuff. I put it in Harry's room."

"Where's Harry sleeping?" I asked.

"Take one guess," said Zoe. She looked at me and
winked.

At around six o'clock, the camera team
arrived with **Mrs. Thornton.**

"Hello, new family," she sang as she walked
through the door. She was carrying huge wrapped
boxes tied with ribbon. She handed a large pink box
to Zoe and a green one to me.

"Where's little Larry?" she asked.

"You mean **Harry**," I said.

Just then Harry rushed in. He grabbed the large
yellow box Mrs. Thornton was holding out to him.

"What do you say?" asked Mrs. Thornton.

"What's for dinner?" asked Harry.

* * *

An hour later, we were sitting at the dining
table eating a SPECIAL pasta dish that
Mrs. Thornton had made.

She wanted us to call her Liz, but after knowing her as Mrs. Thornton for my whole life, **that was going to be hard.**

We were all on our best behavior. **Well, I wasn't.** I was still hoping they'd cancel the show, even if Rose didn't care anymore. But Zoe was **polite** and asked for the pasta recipe. Dad asked Mrs. Thornton about her day. Harry even told her some JOKES to make her feel at home.

It's hard to act *normal* when people are pointing cameras at you. It was making me worry about **everything I did.**

Mrs. Thornton must have been worried too. She was laughing a lot even when there was **nothing funny** to laugh at.

The mothers had each been given a list of things they had to do for the first week. Mrs. Thornton's list was everything that Mom did at home.

I looked at it after Mrs. Thornton stuck it on the fridge and I was a little surprised. I mean, I doubt Mom did all the things on the list. **It was way too long.**

After dinner, I didn't feel like watching TV, so I hung out in my room with Boris. I felt like calling Joe or Bec, but the production people were still hanging around. **I didn't feel like being on TV** while I was on the phone.

I looked at my present from Mrs. Thornton again. It was nice of her to give us something, even if most of it was **free stuff** that she got from her job.

My box of stuff included a hat that said *Serge — We Mean Business* on the front, some STICKERS about a football team, a plastic bottle advertising a sports drink, and a **tiny towel** that went with the bottle.

I started wondering who would use such a tiny towel. Then **Harry** came into my room in his PJs.

"Did you get some **cool stuff**?" he asked.

I nodded and scooped everything into the box. "You?" I asked.

He nodded and **rubbed his eyes.** "I'm going to bed now," he said. He climbed into the sleeping bag that was on top of the blow-up mattress on my floor.

By the time I got into bed, Dad had dropped by and said **goodnight**. I left my light on for a while. Then I realized that Mom wasn't going to come in and kiss me goodnight.

So I **turned off** the light.

CHAPTER 6

JUST WAIT

That first week of *Trading Moms* was **the longest week of my life.**

I knew we weren't **supposed** to talk to Mom, but I kept trying to figure out ways to contact her without anyone knowing.

Joe said he would take her a **message** if I wanted to write her a letter. But writing her a letter sounded too much like **homework**.

Bec said she would call Mom and tell her whatever I wanted to say, but what I really wanted was to **hear Mom's voice.**

It took me a couple of days to get used to seeing **Mrs. Thornton** when I got up in the morning. She was always ℭℋℰℰℛ𝒴 and rushing around saying, "There's just **not enough time in the day** to get all this done." She'd cut back to a couple of hours of work a day so she could be with us in the morning and after school like Mom usually was.

I wondered what MOM was doing at the Thornton house.

I tried to talk to Rose about it, but she'd gone back to her **normal ways** of never talking to me. When I asked her for the hundredth time how Mom was, Rose said, "I'm not really allowed to talk to you about her."

I noticed that Rose didn't ask about her mom.

"Does she have a message for me?" I asked.

"She doesn't really talk about you," said Rose.

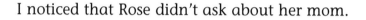

Two mornings after Mrs. Thornton arrived, **Zoe** was **stomping** around looking for her basketball uniform. Finally, she asked Mrs. Thornton where it was.

"I put it in the machine days ago, but it isn't in my closet," said Zoe.

"Machine?" said Mrs. Thornton.

I could see that Zoe was trying to be patient because the cameras were rolling, but **morning is not her favorite time of day.** She usually doesn't talk to anyone until about 10 a.m.

"Washing machine. Washing machine," said Zoe, pointing to the list on the fridge.

Mrs. Thornton peered at the list. "I haven't gotten to that yet," she said. "So, I guess your basketball uniform is **still there.**"

"Arrrgggh," groaned Zoe. She went to the laundry room. A minute later she came back with a slightly **damp**, crumpled uniform.

"You could just pop it in the dryer," offered Mrs. Thornton.

"It SMELLS," complained Zoe.

It did smell. It smelled bad. **I could smell it from where I was standing.**

"Well, you can either dry it or not wear it," said Mrs. Thornton. She was smiling, but it was the kind of smile that **hides a frown** on the inside.

Zoe **stormed off** with her uniform. I heard Irini say, "Did you get a close-up of her face?"

I wondered who she was talking about, Zoe or Mrs. Thornton.

* * *

Harry needed help with his homework that night. Mom was usually the **homework helper**, but Mrs. Thornton pointed out that the list didn't say that she had to do that.

"Besides," she said. "I'm not very good with that kind of thing. Rose usually gets her father to help her."

So **Dad** and Harry stayed up really late trying to make a model of a seascape. It ended up looking more like something that **washed up** on the beach. Dad may have been a scientist, but he was definitely **not good** at art.

Zoe was having TROUBLE putting a zipper in the outfit she was making for her sewing class at school, but Mrs. Thornton couldn't help.

"I usually take things that need sewing to the dry cleaner," Mrs. Thornton said. "Can't you just **staple** it or something?"

Meanwhile, I spent a lot of time not cooperating with **Irini** and the production crew.

It didn't change anything. The cameras kept rolling as I fed Mrs. Thornton's food to the dog and left muddy footprints on the kitchen floor and hid her chores list in the fridge.

Things were getting to the **breaking point** with the family, though. Dad spent a lot of time in the computer room with the door shut. Harry and Zoe couldn't seem to **deal** with not having Mom around.

On the fifth day of *Trading Moms*, **Mrs. Thornton** pulled me into the kitchen before the camera crew had a chance to set up.

"Listen," she said. "I know this is **no fun** for you. I know everyone's mad at me. But I am trying my best. I have never cooked so much in my life, let alone all the other things I have to do around here."

"You just have to last two more days and things are going to get **a lot better** around here," she said. "Just wait and see."

She was looking at me like she wanted an answer or something, so I nodded. Then she left.

Being on TV was **nothing** like I thought it would be.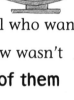

Sure, now there were kids at school who wanted to know my name. Even though the show wasn't going to be on TV for months, **some of them even asked for my autograph.**

Jake Davern wanted to know if I could tell him anything exciting that had happened so far, but nothing had. I was just living with **someone else's mother.** Sometimes I had to go into an empty room, where Irini asked me some questions and I would talk to the camera.

They didn't get much out of me. I pretended I was a super spy being questioned. I only answered with one word, like "nope," "yep," or "maybe."

I was happy to mark off the end of the first week on the kitchen calendar. That's when I noticed a new list stuck on the fridge. The list read *"Thornton's Rules."*

That's when I realized that **everything** was about to change.

CHAPTER 7

THE WORST DAY

The next morning I was in bed when it started raining on my face. Actually, I dreamed it was raining, but really it was **Boris licking my cheek**.

"Good morning, boy," I said.

Then I realized it was the **worst day of the week**. Monday. I knew Dad had already gone to work. He always left early. But Mom hadn't knocked on my door yet, so I figured I had a couple more minutes of time to sleep. I was still lying there when Harry burst through my door.

"You better get up," he said, "or you are going to be **really late**."

Something was wrong. Harry was dressed for school and he already had his backpack on. I hadn't even heard him get up.

"What are you talking about? What time is it?" I asked.

"Time to go," said Harry.

"Where's Mrs. Thornton?" I asked.

"She left already," said Harry. "She had to go to work."

Then I remembered. Thornton's Rules kicked in overnight. Maybe I should have read them.

It only took me five minutes to get dressed, grab something to eat, and get out the door. The camera people were hanging around, drinking coffee, when I burst through my bedroom door. One of them SPILLED his coffee when I ran through the living room.

Harry and I had to **run the whole way** to school. I was almost there when I remembered about my homework. I'd left it on the kitchen table the night before.

"Where was Zoe this morning?" I asked Harry as we ran.

Harry shrugged. "I guess she was in bed," he said.

I didn't think any more about Zoe because I was too busy having **a bad day**.

First, I didn't have my **homework**. Second, I didn't have any **lunch**, because it wasn't sitting on the kitchen table when I left. And third, **Rose Thornton seemed annoyed with me**, even though I hadn't done anything.

I was sitting under the oak tree with Joe and Bec at lunchtime when Rose marched up. She shoved a **brown paper bag** under my nose.

"What?" I said.

"Look what I have to eat," she said.

"Brown paper?" I asked.

"No. Your mother made me lunch. Made it!" Rose yelled. "I usually buy my lunch. **I hate homemade lunches.**"

"If you don't want it, I'll take it," I said hopefully, reaching out for the bag.

Rose snatched the bag away. "I'm going to have to put up with this for four more lunches," she said. "And she made me eat breakfast. I never eat breakfast."

My mouth started watering just
thinking about my mom's breakfasts.

"Well, that sounds AWFUL, Rose,"
said **Bec**, shaking her head.

"I know," said Rose, who didn't get the joke.
"I don't know how I'm going to survive." Then she
tossed her hair and walked away.

* * *

After school, I got home to a very grumpy **Zoe**.
When I say very grumpy, I just mean **more
grumpy than usual.**

"Why didn't you wake me up?" she demanded
as I walked through the front door.

"I was running late," I said. "Anyway, I didn't
figure out you were still in bed until it was too late.
Where's the crew?" I was trying to change the subject.

"Irini called to say they'll be here soon," Zoe said.
"I am really over this, **Dribbles**."

"Don't call me that when the cameras are on,"
I said.

"Sure, **Dribbles**," she said as she walked off to her room.

I raided the pantry for something to eat. If Mom had been home, she would have made me eat a piece of fruit. I ate a whole bag of **chips** and five **chocolate chip cookies**. Then I had a bottle of **soda**. Then I had a **candy bar**.

Maybe not having Mom around wasn't so bad after all.

Harry was watching TV. That's where I found him when Irini and the production crew pulled into the driveway.

"They're here," I said.

Harry nodded glumly. It made me feel **BAD** to see Harry so sad.

"Hey, watch this," I said. Then I turned off the TV and **locked the front door.**

"What are you doing?" asked Harry.

"Just playing a trick," I said. "Come on. **It'll be fun.**"

Then I made Harry **hide** with me behind the  curtains. We watched as the camera crew walked up to the front door and knocked. Harry started to giggle.

"Ssssh," I said.

Then Irini marched up to the door and knocked again. *Really loudly.*

Harry giggled louder. Then he whispered, "What if Zoe lets them in?"

"She'll NEVER hear them," I said. She was in her room listening to music.

Irini **banged** loudly on the door again. Then she marched to her van, dug around for a while, and came back to the front door.

"What is she doing?" asked Harry.

I couldn't believe it. "She has a key," I said.

Then the front door opened.

* * *

Dad got home about an hour later. He looked a little tired, but he **smiled** at me and Harry. "How's it going, boys?" he asked.

I just shrugged. The extra camera lighting in the house was making my eyes hurt.

"What's for dinner?" said Dad, sniffing at the air.

I don't know what he was sniffing at. There was nothing cooking in the kitchen.

"No one is making dinner," I said. **"The rules have all changed."**

"And I need help with my homework," said Harry.

Dad looked sad.

"Six days to go, Dad," I said.

It was going to be a long six days.

CHAPTER 8

THORNTON'S RULES

Before Mrs. Thornton got home, I read her list to Harry.

Thornton's Rules

1. I will be leaving the house at 6:00 a.m. Each family member is responsible for getting out of bed on time, unless you wish to be woken up when I leave.

2. Breakfast is self-serve. Please stack your dishes in the dishwasher. Turn on the dishwasher if it is full.

3. Please put your dirty clothes straight into the washing machine. If it is full, turn it on. (Keep whites with whites, and colors go in a separate wash.)

4. If there are wet clothes in the washing machine, please put them in the dryer.

5. I will return home from work at 7:00 p.m. each day.

6. I will organize dinner.

7. The dog is to stay outside or in the laundry room.

8. TV should only be watched after all homework is completed.

9. The same goes for Internet access and phone.

10. Let's have fun!

"Is she kidding?" asked Harry. "No TV?"

"Wait until Zoe reads this," I said. "She is going to FREAK OUT."

Then the phone rang. I wasn't sure whether I could answer it, because I hadn't done my homework yet. I answered it anyway. It was Mrs. Thornton.

"David, I'm just calling to see what you'd like me to pick up for dinner. Chicken? Pizza? Chinese?" she said.

"Are you serious?" I asked. I cheered. Then I told her definitely pizza.

"Okay, Harry," I said after I hung up. "Dinner is on the way. Let's check out this list again."

Harry nodded.

"You do the **dishwasher**," I said. "I'll check the washing machine."

"What about Zoe?" asked Harry.

We couldn't decide who should talk to Zoe. We even asked Irini if she would, but **she just got mad** and told us we had to pretend the production people weren't there.

In the end, we decided to leave Zoe in her room. Hopefully she wasn't on the Internet, because I was sure she hadn't done her **homework**.

I left Harry in the kitchen. He was putting the last dishes into the dishwasher. I checked the washing machine. Sure enough, **it had clothes in it.**

There were some more clothes in the hamper. I put them in too. Then I turned on the machine and closed the laundry room door.

- 57 -

"How's that dishwasher going, Harry?" I asked.

Harry gave me a thumbs-up. "Good," he said.

"Hello, **new family**," a voice called from the front door. "I need some help, please."

Just then, Boris waddled into the kitchen. He must have smelled the pizza all the way from my bedroom.

"Quick, put **Boris** in the laundry room," I told Harry. I went to help Mrs. Thornton.

That night we had a great dinner. I pushed my crusts to one my side of my plate (I usually fed them to Boris under the table, but he was in the laundry room). I got to drink as much soda as I wanted.

Mom never let us have soda for dinner.

After we ate, I offered to take the plates to the kitchen. Zoe and Mrs. Thornton talked about the latest album by Silver Side. I had no idea who they were. I was pretty sure that Mom wouldn't know them either. Zoe and Mrs. Thornton seemed to be getting along.

Even Dad seemed happy.

I thought **MAYBE** the rest of the week wasn't going to be so bad.

Then I reached the kitchen. I put the plates down and called Harry in to help me.

"Whoa!" he said as he came in.

"**Shut the door** behind you," I whispered.

Too late. A cameraman had followed us into the kitchen.

"Whoa," Harry said again.

"What did you put in the dishwasher?" I asked.

"Dishes," said Harry.

"How much **powder** did you put in?" I asked.

"Powder?" Harry said. He pulled out a bottle of green liquid. "I put this in."

Harry had put **hand soap** in the dishwasher. I was standing **knee-deep in suds.** How could we clean it up without Mrs. Thornton finding out?

"Are you getting this? **This is great**," someone said. It was Irini. She was really starting to get on my nerves.

"This is **really cool**," said Harry. He jumped into a large pile of suds.

"Help me get rid of it," I said.

I tried pushing the bubbles **down the kitchen sink.** That didn't work.

Harry tried shoving the bubbles in his sweater and taking them outside. Then he put some in a pot and **tried to melt them.**

Then Mrs. Thornton finally came in. She took one look at the floor, covered with bubbles, and just **told us to fix it.**

Harry and I were $\mathbb{SHOCKED}$. Mom would have had a fit.

Then we all sat down to watch our **favorite** TV show. First, we told Mrs. Thornton we'd done our homework. I'd definitely **thought** about doing my homework, so I thought that was good enough.

It must have been too **boring** for the production people, because they left early.

All in all it wasn't a bad day. I asked Dad to wake me up before he left the next morning. Then I snuck **Boris** into my room when I went to bed.

Right before I fell asleep, I had the feeling I'd **forgotten** to do something.

The last thing I heard was Boris snoring.

CHAPTER 9

DISASTER!

The next couple of days were okay. It's not like I wasn't missing Mom, but we did get to have **fast food** for dinner. Also, **Mrs. Thornton** brought home lots of presents from all the people she worked for.

She wasn't around a lot. I guess she was really **busy** at work. When she was at my house, she seemed nice enough.

Zoe was mad about the whole Internet/homework thing. But she was **really happy** when Mrs. Thornton gave her some tickets to the Bays Park International Fashion Extravaganza.

On Wednesday night, Harry wanted to talk about what we would do with our **$50,000**.

"I think we should build **a swimming pool** in our back yard," he said.

"With a **huge** slide that's fifty feet tall and goes around and around?" I asked.

"Yeah," said Harry.

"Harry, you hated that slide when we went to Grand Mountain Water Park," I said.

Harry frowned. "I was just a kid then," he said.

I didn't bother to point out that **he was still just a kid.**

"Maybe we could set up a home theater," said Harry. "That would be 𝗌o cool."

I nodded.

The production people were eating dinner.  They had **hamburgers** and **fries.**

"What's for dinner?" Harry asked me.

That made me think of the *Thornton's Rules* list on the fridge.

"Have you filled the dishwasher, Harry?" I asked.

Harry shrugged. "I did it last night," he said.

"What about today?" I asked.

"I have to do it today too?" he whined. **"That's not fair."**

Then I thought about the laundry I'd done on Monday. "You'd better fill the dishwasher before Mrs. Thornton gets home," I said. Then I RACED to the laundry room.

Sure enough, the laundry that I'd done on Monday night was still in the washing machine. I quickly pulled the clothes out. Then I shoved them into the dryer.

I heard the front door bang. Mrs. Thornton was home. Then I realized **Boris was inside,** but it was too late to put him in the laundry room.

Mrs. Thornton was frowning as she put her laptop and briefcase on the kitchen table.

"Has the dishwasher been filled?" she asked.

"Yup," said Harry. "What's for dinner?"

"Well, I had a very nice day, **thank you, Larry,**" said Mrs. Thornton with a frown.

"It's Harry," said **Harry**.

But **Mrs. Thornton wasn't listening.**
She was too busy ordering Chinese food.

"David, could you bring my other briefcase in
from the **back seat** of my car?" asked Mrs.
Thornton with the phone to her ear. She handed
me the keys to her car.

Mrs. Thornton had a nice car. It was *silver* and
sporty and low to the ground. It had a
sunroof and shiny wheels.

I'd never been in her car before, so I slid behind the
wheel to look at the **really cool dashboard.**
It had a GPS and a MP3 sound system.

I turned the lights on so I could get a closer look
at the controls. **The dashboard lit up like an
airplane cockpit.**

"Good evening, ladies and gentlemen," I said.
"This is your captain, David Mortimore Baxter,
speaking. Please keep your seatbelts on until I say so.
Also, we will be serving dinner shortly."

Dinner! I could see the Chinese food delivery van pull up behind me. I really *don't know* how I knocked the brake off. One minute, the car was sitting still in the driveway.  The next minute, it was **rolling back** into the delivery van.

It hit the van and shuddered to a stop. The CRUNCH sounded like I'd run over a can of soda.

Luckily, a cameraman had followed me outside. He **kept filming** while the deliveryman got out of his van and started yelling.

Mrs. Thornton was pretty nice about the **dent in her car**. She said it could have happened to anyone. I told her I'd pay for it out of my allowance, but she said not to bother because that's what car insurance was for. Then Harry pointed out that she probably wasn't covered by car insurance because I had been at the wheel.

Mrs. Thornton changed the subject. The cameras kept rolling.

I wondered where Boris was hiding. Mrs. Thornton yelled at him every single time she saw him in the house.

"I have a breakfast meeting tomorrow morning," said Mrs. Thornton. "*Has the laundry been done?* I'll need my white shirt."

I nodded. "It's in the dryer," I said.

Two minutes later, I could hear Mrs. Thornton's SCREECH all the way in the kitchen.

I ran to the laundry room. A cameraman followed me. I expected Boris to be **slobbering** all over Mrs. Thornton, or something. But Boris wasn't there. **Mrs. Thornton** was standing in the middle of the laundry room, holding up something pink.

"What's that?" I asked.

Mrs. Thornton opened her mouth a few times and closed it a few times. **She looked like Harry's fish did when it jumped out of the fish tank and landed on the carpet.**

"White shirt," she said finally.

I shook my head. "That's not a white shirt," I said. "It's **PINK**."

"White! Shirt!" said Mrs. Thornton.

She held out the pink cloth. It looked like a shirt for a **baby**.

"It's not white," I said. "And it's really little. It's — oh."

Mrs. Thornton had reached into the dryer and pulled out a red sock.

"Whites together, colors together," she said. "You put my good white shirt in the laundry with this **DISGUSTING** old red sock. And then you put it in the dryer. Didn't you look at the label? You shrunk my shirt!"

Her voice was getting **louder** and **louder**. Zoe and Harry came to see what was wrong. I could see Irini's face at the door. She looked really **HAPPY**.

Suddenly I didn't care about the money anymore. I wanted *Trading Moms* to be over. **I wanted my mother to come home.**

That's when Mrs. Thornton screamed again. I turned and saw Boris casually waddling in. He had Mrs. Thornton's **underwear** on his head and a tube of lipstick sticking out of his mouth.

CHAPTER 10

SICK OF IT

There were four days left. I didn't think I could make it. I just wanted things to go **back to normal**.

I wanted my bedroom back to myself. I wanted to come home from school and have **Mom** 𝕹𝕬𝕲𝕲𝕴𝕹𝕲 me about the homework I'd forgotten to take to school. I wanted Mom to come into my room at night and tell me it was time to turn off my light.

I didn't want to **worry** about what laundry went with what. I didn't want to worry that Harry was going to turn the kitchen into a **huge soap bubble** by putting in the wrong soap.

I held a meeting in my bedroom. We couldn't have it in Harry's room because that was Mrs. Thornton's room. And we couldn't have it in Zoe's room because that was **off limits** to everyone except Zoe.

Zoe, Harry, and Boris sat on my bed. I shoved my desk chair under the door handle to keep everyone else out.

"The cameras are supposed to have access to us at **all times**," said Zoe.

"That's another thing I'm sick of," I said. "I'm sick of always having a camera **shoved in my face.** And when they aren't doing that, they're sneaking around behind our backs just waiting for us to do something STUPID."

"Yeah," Harry said.

"**It's not personal**," said Zoe. "They're just doing their jobs."

"Well, they can do it somewhere else," I said. "It's just like Rose said before this all started. Everyone's going to **laugh** at us. I don't want to do it anymore."

"There's nothing we can do," said Zoe. "Dad signed the contract. We can't back out now. There are only four days left. Two of those days are the weekend. I think we just have to **hang in there**. For Dad's sake. I know he feels really bad about the whole thing. It was his idea to do this."

"I can't believe he did this just for the **money**," I said.

"I don't think he did," said Zoe. "You know what he's like. He thought it would be an **interesting experiment** for the whole family. But we're not lab rats and this isn't his laboratory."

"But Mom did it for the money. That just doesn't seem like her," I said.

The doorknob rattled. "David?" Irini said.

"I'm changing clothes," I yelled.

"Four more days," Zoe whispered.

"Four days," I replied. But I still didn't know if I could make it.

* * *

I had a meeting with Rose in the library the next day to see how the Thornton household was holding up. Rose had a list of her own complaints about the show.

1. She hadn't had takeout all week, since Baxter Rules had kicked in.

2. My mom made her go to bed too early on school nights.

3. Mom had cooked something called veggie loaf, which was disgusting.

4. Mom wouldn't let Rose watch TV in her room.

5. Rose had been grounded on the first day of Baxter Rules because she hadn't come home right away after school.

"I don't think she can **ground** me," Rose said. "Coming home right away after school was one of her rules, but that doesn't make her the **boss** of me. My mother is going to be **absolutely furious** when she finds out."

"Uh huh," I said.

"And she makes me turn off the light at nine o'clock," Rose said. "Like I'm **a little kid** or something. Everyone knows that all of the good TV shows start at 9:30."

I nodded, but inside I was secretly pleased. Something good had come out of all this. **My mom grounded Rose Thornton.**

"And I'm really **SICK** of the cameras following me around," said Rose. "If I let them, they'd follow me into the bathroom!"

That made me laugh. But then I noticed that **Rose's** eyes were **leaking** like she was crying or something.

"Hey," I said. I didn't know what to say, because:

a) **A girl was crying.**

b) **This was not just any girl. This was Rose Thornton, my biggest enemy.**

I tried to cheer her up and tell her some **JOKES**, but that just made her cry more.

"I just want my mom to come home," said Rose. "I really miss her."

"You do?" I said.

Rose nodded.

"Well, I don't think you miss her half as much as she misses you," I said, even though Mrs. Thornton had **not once** mentioned Rose.

"Really?" said Rose.

"Sure," I said. "She never stops talking about you. I'm sick of it. **Rose, Rose, Rose.** I had to ask her to stop."

"Really?" said Rose. She stopped crying.

I nodded and said, "Sure. Anyway, there's only a couple of days left. I usually feed Mom's veggie loaf to the dog when she's not looking. Do you have a **dog?** Or a **rabbit** maybe?"

Rose shook her head. So then we talked about how Rose could get the veggie loaf from the table to the trash or outside under a bush without my mom seeing. We came up with such **crazy solutions** that Rose ended up laughing.

Then it was the end of lunchtime. I realized that I'd spent the whole time hanging out with Rose instead of my friends.

And it hadn't been that bad at all.

* * *

The next four days couldn't go fast enough. Then all of a sudden we were CROWDED into the dining room for a final filming with **Mrs. Thornton.**

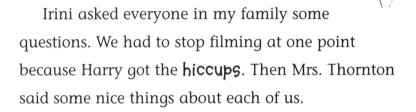

Irini asked everyone in my family some questions. We had to stop filming at one point because Harry got the hiccups. Then Mrs. Thornton said some nice things about each of us.

She didn't once mention the car or the shirt or the fact that Boris had gotten into her things. She said she hoped that we'd learned something from having her in our home.

Then Dad made a nice speech and Irini called it a wrap.

The next morning was **mom-swap time.** I was never so glad to see Mom coming through the front door. And I could tell **she was glad to be home**, too.

"Who left their bike outside?" she said.

Then we all jumped on her for a hug. The camera lights shined brightly over us like a **friendly** sun.

"Did you get that?" I heard Irini ask a cameraman.

Then Irini told us that the Thornton parents and the Baxter parents would have to have one final meeting.

Then that was **THE END** of *Trading Moms*.

CHAPTER 11

THE PRIZE

But that wasn't the end of it. Two days later, Dad got a call to say the show had been **canceled**. But they told him we would still get our **prize money**.

"Sorry, kids," said **Dad**, "but you aren't going to be on TV."

Harry cheered and Boris started barking.

"That's good," said Zoe. "I was a little **nervous** to see myself on TV."

"So what are we going to spend our  money on?" asked Harry.

Mom reminded us that it was up to her to decide what we would spend the money on. We all made a few suggestions, but she shook her head.

"I already decided," she said. "In fact, I'd decided the day I agreed to do the show."

"You did?" I asked.

Mom nodded.

"So?" said Zoe.

"So, before I tell you, I want you to tell me what you've learned about this **experience**," said Mom.

"I learned that I never want to sleep in David's room again," said **Harry**. "He snores."

"I learned that you do a lot of stuff we didn't know about," said **Zoe**.

"I learned that it was **a bad idea**," said Dad.

Mom laughed. "It wasn't all bad," she said. Then she looked at me. "What about you, David?"

"I learned that white clothes don't go into the washing machine with colored clothes," I said. "And I also learned that you have to be CAREFUL what you put in the dryer."

Mom nodded.

"And I wouldn't trade moms again for **all the money in the world**," I added.

Mom smiled. "That's *sweet*, David," she said.

"So what are we doing with the money?" squealed Harry.

"We're donating it to **charity**," said **Mom.**

"What?" said Harry.

"No!" I said.

"What did she say?" asked Zoe.

"What charity?" said Dad.

"The Bays Park Historical Society," said Mom.

* * *

Later, when I talked to **Joe**, he asked me what I thought the coolest thing in the world was, now that **being on TV** was off my list. I had to think about that for a while.

"You know, Joe," I finally said, "I think the coolest thing in the world is **being a Baxter**."

About the Author

When Karen Tayleur was growing up, her father told
her many stories about his own childhood. These
stories continued to grow. She says, "I always enjoyed
the retelling, and wanted to create a character who
had the same abilities with 'bending the truth.'" And
David Mortimore Baxter was born! Karen lives in
Australia with her husband, two children, two cats,
and one dog.

About the Illustrator

Brann Garvey lives in Minneapolis, Minnesota with
his wife, Keegan, their dog, Lola, and their very fat
cat, Iggy. Brann graduated from Iowa State University
with a bachelor of fine arts degree. He later attended
the Minneapolis College of Art and Design, where
he studied illustration. In his free time, Brann enjoys
being with his family and friends. He brings his
sketchbook everywhere he goes.

Glossary

autograph (AW-tuh-graf)—a person's signature

charity (CHA-ruh-tee)—an organization that raises money for a good cause

complicated (KOM-pli-kay-tid)—containing lots of different parts and ideas and very hard to understand

cooperating (koh-OP-ur-ayt-ing)—working together

crew (KROO)—a team of people who work together

documentaries (dok-yuh-MEN-tuh-reez)—movies made about real situations and people

editor (ED-uh-tur)—a person who checks the contents of a TV show and gets it ready to be shown

experiment (ek-SPER-uh-ment)—a scientific test to try something out

obvious (OB-vee-uhss)—easy to see or understand

producer (pruh-DOOSS-ur)—a person in charge of making a movie or TV show

production people (pruh-DUHK-shuhn PEE-puhl)—the production people work behind the scenes on a TV show

reality show (ree-AL-uh-tee SHOW)—a TV show about real people and situations

revenge (ri-VENJ)—action that you take to pay someone back for harm the person has done to you

Discussion Questions

1. Why do David and Rose plan to try to stop the show? Why does Rose change her mind? What else could they have done if they were unhappy about the show?

2. David's family follows their own rules for the first week, and Mrs. Thornton's rules for the second week. Which week do you think was better? Why?

3. What would be good about being on TV? What would be bad about it? Talk about your answers.

Writing Prompts

1. If you had to be on a reality show, which show would you choose to be on? Write about what you think it would be like.

2. Pretend that your family has traded one member with another family. Who did you trade? What would be different in your life if that person was gone for a week?

3. From reading this book, you know what David's experience on *Trading Moms* was like. What was Rose's like? Write about what you think happened at the Thornton house.

Spies! **DAVID MORTIMORE BAXTER** by Karen Tayleur

DAVID MORTIMORE BAXTER Excuses! by Karen Tayleur

DAVID MORTIMORE BAXTER Chic... by Karen T...

David Mortimore Baxter

David is a great kid, but he has one big problem — he can't stop talking. These wildly humorous stories, told by David himself, will show readers just how much trouble a boy and his mouth can get into, whether he's going on a class trip, trying to find a missing neighbor, running a detective agency, or getting lost in the wild. David is amiable, engaging, cool, and smart enough to realize that growing up is the biggest adventure of all.

With David!

Haunted!

GET LOST WITH DAVID MORTIMORE BAXTER

DAVID MORTIMORE BAXTER
Wild!
by KAREN TAYLOR

Internet Sites

Do you want to know more about subjects related to this book? Or are you interested in learning about other topics? Then check out FactHound, a fun, easy way to find Internet sites.

Our investigative staff has already sniffed out great sites for you!

Here's how to use FactHound:

1. Visit *www.facthound.com*

2. Select your grade level.

3. To learn more about subjects related to this book, type in the book's ISBN number: 9781434211965.

4. Click the **Fetch It** button.

FactHound will fetch the best Internet sites for you!